Parents and Caregivers,

Here are a few ways to support your beginning reader:

- Talk with your child about the ideas addressed in the story.
- Discuss each illustration, mentioning the characters, where they are, and what they are doing.
- Read with expression, pointing to each word.
- Talk about why the character did what he or she did and what your child would do in that situation.
- Help your child connect with characters and events in the story.

Remember, reading with your child should be fun, not forced.

Gail Saunders-Smith, Ph.D

Padres y personas que cuidan niños,

Aquí encontrarán algunas formas de apoyar al lector que recién se inicia:

- Hable con su niño/a sobre las ideas desarrolladas en el cuento.
- Discuta cada ilustración, mencionando los personajes, dónde se encuentran y qué están haciendo.
- Lea con expresión, señalando cada palabra.
- Hable sobre por qué el personaje hizo lo que hizo y qué haría su niño/a en esa situación.
- Ayude al niño/a a conectarse con los personajes y los eventos del cuento.

Recuerde, leer con su hijo/a debe ser algo divertido, no forzado.

Gail Saunders-Smith, Ph.D

BILINGUAL STONE ARCH READERS

are published by Stone Arch Books, a Capstone imprint
1710 Roe Crest Drive, North Mankato, Minnesota 56003
www.capstonepub.com

Library of Congress Cataloging-in-Publication data is available on the
Library of Congress website.

ISBN: 978-1-4342-3781-1 (hardcover)
ISBN: 978-1-4342-3920-4 (paperback)

Art Director: Bob Lentz
Graphic Designer: Hilary Wacholz
Original Translation: Claudia Heck
Translation Services: Strictly Spanish
Reading Consultants: Gail Saunders-Smith, Ph.D; Melinda Melton Crow, M.Ed;
Laurie K. Holland, Media Specialist

Printed in the United States of America in North Mankato, Minnesota.
042018   000381

LA GRAN PESCA
THE BIG CATCH

Un cuento sobre Robot y Rico

A Robot and Rico Story

por/by Anastasia Suen
ilustrado por/illustrated by Mike Laughead

STONE ARCH BOOKS
a capstone imprint

WITHDRAWN

This is ROBOT. Robot has lots of tools. He uses the tools to help his best friend, Rico.

Este es ROBOT. Robot tiene muchas herramientas. Él usa las herramientas para ayudar a su mejor amigo, Rico.

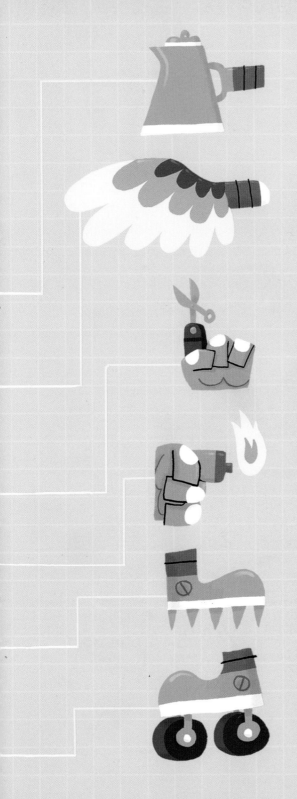

Teapot/
Tetera

Wings/
Alas

Scissors/
Tijeras

Fire Finger/
Dedo de fuego

Special Shoes/
Zapatos especiales

Roller Skates/
Patines con ruedas

Robot and Rico are at the beach.
"I will catch a big one," says Rico.

Robot y Rico están en la playa.
"Pescaré uno grande", dice Rico.

"How big?" asks Robot.
"We will see," says Rico.

"¿Cuán grande?" pregunta Robot.
"Veremos", dice Rico.

"Now I will take a short nap,"
says Rico.

"Ahora dormiré una siesta corta",
dice Rico.

"This is boring," says Robot.

"Esto es aburrido", dice Robot.

Robot walks down the beach.
"What are you doing?" Robot asks
a little girl.

Robot camina por la playa.
"¿Qué haces?" Robot pregunta
a una niña.

"I am making a sand castle,"
she says.
"I can do that," says Robot.

"Estoy haciendo un castillo de arena",
dice ella.
"Yo lo puedo hacer", dice Robot.

Tug! Tug! Rico wakes up.

¡Tirón! ¡Tirón! Rico se despierta.

"It's a big one!" says Rico.
"Help me, Robot."

"¡Es uno grande!" dice Rico.
"Ayúdame, Robot".

Robot and Rico pull the line in.
"It's a boot," says Rico. "Throw it back."

Robot y Rico recogen la línea.
"Es una bota", dice Rico.
"Tírala al agua".

14

"No," says Robot. "I can use it."
Robot takes the boot off the hook.

"No", dice Robot. "Puedo usarla".
Robot saca la bota del anzuelo.

Rico throws the line out again.
He takes a nap.

Rico lanza la línea de nuevo.
Él toma una siesta.

"I can dig with this boot," says Robot. "Now I can make a really big sand castle."

"Puedo cavar con esta bota", dice Robot. "Ahora puedo hacer un castillo de arena bien grande".

Tug! Tug! Rico wakes up.

¡Tirón! ¡Tirón! Rico se despierta.

"It's a big one!" says Rico.
"Help me, Robot."

"¡Es uno grande!" dice Rico.
"Ayúdame, Robot".

They pull the line in.
"It's a tire," says Rico.
"Throw it back."

Ellos recogen la línea.
"Es una llanta", dice Rico.
"Tírala al agua".

"No," says Robot. "I can use it."
Robot takes the tire off the hook.

"No", dice Robot. "Puedo usarla".
Robot saca la llanta del anzuelo.

21

Rico throws the line out again.
He takes another short nap.

Rico lanza la línea de nuevo.
Él toma otra siesta corta.

Robot puts the tire in the sand.
"My sand castle is getting big,"
says Robot.

Robot pone la llanta en la arena.
"Mi castillo de arena se está
agrandando", dice Robot.

24

Tug! Tug!
"It's a big one!" says Rico.
"Help me, Robot."

¡Tirón! ¡Tirón!
"¡Es uno grande!" dice Rico.
"Ayúdame, Robot".

"It is a big one," says Robot.
The puffer fish grows and grows!
"And it keeps getting bigger,"
says Rico.

"Es uno grande", dice Robot.
¡El pez globo crece y crece!
"Y cada vez es más grande",
dice Rico.

"But we cannot eat it," says Rico.
"Throw it back," says Robot.

"Pero no podemos comerlo", dice Rico.
"Tíralo al agua", dice Robot.

"Good-bye, big fish!" they say.
"Now what?" asks Rico.

"¡Adiós, pez grande!" dicen ellos.
"¿Y ahora qué?" dice Rico.

"You can help me build my
sand castle. It's a big one,"
says Robot.
"The biggest," says Rico.

"Puedes ayudarme a construir mi
castillo de arena. Es grande",
dice Robot.
"El más grande", dice Rico.

story words

beach   sand castle   tire

nap   hook   throw

palabras del cuento

playa   castillo de arena   llanta

siesta   anzuelo   tirar